THE GARAGE

PHILIPPE DUPASQUIER

WALKER BOOKS
LONDON

Early in the morning, on the way to work,
something goes wrong with John Walker's car.
He leaves it outside the garage.

The garage is not open yet.

Mr Fingers arrives, with Mick and Mack, the mechanics, and Pete, the petrol pump attendant.

Pete tries to start Mr Walker's car, but it
won't go. 'Push it, lads!' Mr Fingers says.
Beryl opens up the shop.

The car transporter arrives, with new cars
for Mr Fingers to sell.

Mick and Mack start work on Mr Walker's car.
Pete serves his first customer.

'My mum would like that car,' Jimmy says to
his schoolfriends.
'Slowly now!' says Mr Fingers.

'This car is a real wreck,' Mick says.
'That will be £10.47p,' Beryl says to the
customer, who counts out the money.

Graham Slick puts air in his tyres.
The petrol tanker delivers petrol.

Everyone is hard at work, which makes
Mr Fingers happy.

Graham's girlfriend, Molly, opens her umbrella,
but it blows inside out.

'What a downpour!' Mack says.
'It's just a passing shower,' says Beryl.

The break-down truck brings in a crashed car.

'Straight ahead!' says Mr Fingers.
'Here comes another one!' Mick says.

'Whoops!' says George. 'Look at my tyre!'
But everyone is looking at the crashed car.

'I skidded right off the road,' the driver
tells Mick. Mr Walker comes to collect his car.
Beryl locks up the shop.

Mr Walker drives away, very pleased that his car has been mended.

Mick gives Mack a lift home on his bike.
Mr Fingers is the last to leave.

Oh dear, Mr Fingers, what a way to end
a busy day!